SONIC THE HEDGEHOG™

ROBOTNIK'S REVENGE

BY

MICHAEL

TEITELBAUM

INTERIOR

ILLUSTRATIONS BY

GLEN HANSON

Troll Associates

Nicholas Pilbeam

Teitelbaum, Michael.
  Sonic The Hedgehog : Robotnik's Revenge / by Michael Teitelbaum ;
interior illustrations by Glen Hanson.
        p. cm.
  Summary : Sonic, a blue super-fast hedgehog, and his Uncle Chuck once
again confront Robotnik and his evil robots.
  ISBN 0-8167-3438-0 (pbk.)
  [1. Hedgehogs — Fiction. 2. Robots — Fiction. 3. Science fiction.]
I. Hanson, Glen, ill.   II. Title.
PZ7. T233Sr   1994
[Fic] — dc20   93–48920

Published by Troll Associates, Inc.

Printed in the United States of America.

10 9 8 7 6 5 4

Produced by Creative Media Applications, Inc.
Art direction by Fabia Wargin.
Cover art by Greg Wray.

This book is dedicated to Adam, Ari, Matthew, and Andrew.

Special thanks to Roy Wandelmaier, Bob Harris, Cynthia Wilkes,
Susan Reyes, Cristina Tuason, Arlene Scanlan, and Diane Drosnes.

Chapter

1

The planet Mobius was once a wonderful place to live. It was filled with happy people, and it was ruled by a kind king. The air was clean and the water was crystal clear.

But not anymore. Things have changed since the evil Dr. Robotnik kidnapped the king and made himself the dictator of Mobius.

Now all is dark and dreary on Mobius. Dr. Robotnik's factories pollute the air and water. Books, music, and fun have all been outlawed.

One by one the citizens of Mobius, called Mobians, are being captured. They are brought to Robotnik's fortress in a city called Robotropolis. There they are put into Robotnik's Ro-Bo-Machine, where they are turned into mindless robotic servants.

Few Mobians walk freely anymore. Those that do must always be on their guard, or they risk capture by Robotnik's patrolling swatbots. Fear has a tight grip over the entire planet.

• • • • •

Deep within Robotropolis, Dr. Robotnik sat in his master control room. On his shoulder stood his pet robot chicken, Cluck. Robotnik surveyed the landscape of Mobius on a bank of video monitors. It was gray and dismal, thanks to Robotnik.

"Lovely, isn't it, Cluck?" asked Robotnik in his deep booming voice.

Cluck snarled. His sinister mechanical growl revealed razor-sharp teeth.

"And it's all mine," cackled Robotnik, petting Cluck with his thick glove. "I created this wonderful wasteland. This gorgeous gray planet."

Robotnik slowly rose from his chair. He looked like a giant egg as he waddled across the room. He stopped in front of a large window. Cluck stretched his metal wings, then settled back down.

"I have changed the planet's landscape," said Robotnik. "I have taken over the government. But I will not rest until every happy, fun-loving Mobian is my robotic servant."

Robotnik peered through the window into a huge room. A large group of captured Mobians huddled there in fear.

In the center of the room a swatbot strapped a small raccoon into a large chair. The raccoon struggled and cried out, but he was no match for the swatbot.

A glass dome dropped from the ceiling, covering the raccoon and the chair. Blue rings of light flashed and a loud hum filled the room. Robotnik's dreaded Ro-Bo-Machine went to work.

The humming and the lights stopped. When the glass dome lifted, the raccoon was unstrapped

from the chair. But it was no longer a raccoon. It was now a robot.

"I-live-to-serve-Robotnik," said the newly formed robot in a mechanical voice.

One by one, all the Mobians in the room were placed in the machine and transformed into robots.

Robotnik laughed. "Excellent. Everything is proceeding according to my plan."

Suddenly, the door to Robotnik's control room burst open. In stumbled Snively, Robotnik's assistant. He was carrying a large stack of papers.

"Pardon me, Dr. Robotnik, sir," began Snively. "I—"

"SNIVELY!" bellowed Robotnik. "What did I tell you about knocking?"

"I'm sorry, sir, but this is very import—"

"Go out and come back in," ordered Robotnik. "And this time do it right!"

"But I—"

"Do it!"

Snively left the room. A few seconds later he knocked again.

"Who is it?" asked Robotnik.

"It is I, sir," said the timid voice from the other side of the door. "Your humble servant, Snively."

"That's better," said Robotnik. "You may enter."

As Snively stepped into the room, Cluck leaped from Robotnik's shoulder. He flapped his wings in Snively's face, causing Snively to drop his papers. Reports, maps, and diagrams scattered all over the floor.

"Get away from me, you stupid chicken!" yelled Snively as he bent down to pick up the papers.

"Now, now, Snively," said Robotnik. "We must not be rude to my faithful friend Cluck."

"But, sir, I thought *I* was your faithful friend," said Snively as he picked up the last of the papers.

"You, Snively, are my fumbling fool," said Robotnik.

"Thank you, sir," said Snively.

"Now," continued Robotnik, "what was so important that you had to interrupt me?"

"I've just received the latest report from your network of spies, sir," said Snively. "They have discovered that your sworn enemy Sonic The Hedgehog has joined Princess Sally's band of Freedom Fighters."

Robotnik's face turned red with rage.

"WHAT?" he bellowed. "Oh, how I HATE THAT HEDGEHOG!"

Robotnik paced back and forth. "This is bad news indeed," he grumbled. "I've never had to worry about that silly band of so-called Freedom Fighters before."

"Princess Sally's attempts to rescue her father, the king, have always been stopped easily, as you well know, sir," added Snively.

"But now," continued Robotnik, "with Sonic and his speed, and those magic power rings on their side, these troublemakers pose a greater threat to me. I need a plan."

"Perhaps, sir," said Snively, "you could capture one of the weaker Freedom Fighters to use as bait to lure Sonic into a trap."

"Shut up, Snively!" said Robotnik. "I'm thinking. I know! I will capture one of the weaker Freedom Fighters to use as bait to lure Sonic into a trap."

"Good plan, sir," sighed Snively.

Robotnik smiled. "Then I will crush that meddling hedgehog once and for all!"

Chapter
2

ZOOM!

Sonic The Hedgehog streaked across the barren plains of Mobius.

"Almost there," he said to himself.

Sonic headed for a lush, green forest. It gave him a welcome break from the empty wastelands he had been patrolling.

Once inside the Great Forest, Sonic breathed a sigh of relief. *I don't have to worry about swatbots in here,* he thought.

The Great Forest was one of the few places on Mobius that had not yet been touched by Robotnik's evil.

Sonic came to a large stump in the forest. Lifting a hidden latch, he raised the top of the stump and jumped into the opening.

"Knothole Village, here I come!" shouted Sonic.

Down he slid, gliding along the twisting slide. The stump and the slide served as the secret entrance to Knothole Village—the underground home of Princess Sally's Freedom Fighters.

"Wheee!" yelled Sonic as he landed in a soft pile of hay. "Way past cool!"

The other Freedom Fighters were waiting for him.

"Report please, Sonic," said Sally.

"Oh, come on, Sal," said Sonic. "You're always so serious."

"Sonic," began Sally, "if we're ever going to free Mobius and put my father back on his rightful throne, we've *got* to be serious. Now please report."

"No sweat, Sal," replied Sonic. "Everything is clear within a fifteen-mile radius. No sign of swatbots and no sign of Robotnik."

At the mention of Robotnik's name, Sonic's

Uncle Chuck and Sonic's faithful dog Muttski, who were both once robotic captives of Robotnik, grew frightened.

"What's wrong, Uncle Chuck?" asked Sonic.

"Just hearing Robotnik's name brings back bad memories," explained Uncle Chuck.

Uncle Chuck was a great inventor. He created Sonic's magic power rings. He and Muttski had been captured by Robotnik and turned into robots. Sonic and Sally risked their lives in a daring rescue mission to free them. After the rescue, Sonic used his magic power rings to change Uncle Chuck and Muttski from robots back to normal.

"Don't worry, Uncle Chuck," said Sonic. "We'll stop Robotnik. Then nobody on Mobius will ever be changed into a robot again."

"Hello, Sonic," came a booming voice.

"Hey, Rotor," said Sonic. "What are you working on?"

Rotor, the sea lion, was a terrific handyman and tinker. He could build or fix anything. He stood next to Sonic, holding wires and dials in one hand and a bunch of tools in the other.

"I've been working on a portable swatbot detector," said Rotor. "Now when we go on patrol, we'll know about *them* before they know about us!"

"Way past cool, Rotor!" shouted Sonic.

"Sonic?" came a meek voice from behind the hedgehog.

"Tails!" said Sonic, turning around. "What's up, little guy?"

Tails was a young fox with two tails. Sonic was his hero. The only thing Tails wanted was to be as brave and fast as Sonic when he grew up.

"Sonic, can I go out on patrol with you next time?" asked Tails.

Sonic didn't want to hurt his little friend's feelings. "I still think you're a bit young. But soon, little guy. Soon."

Tails smiled a big bright smile. He ran off to dream of the day when he would go with Sonic on a dangerous mission.

"Sonic," said Sally. "I think it's time we got down to business. We've got to plan—"

"Howdy, y'all!" interrupted Bunnie Rabbit. "Hey,

Sonic, honey, it's good to see you. What's everybody up to?"

"We were trying to plan tomorrow's scouting missions, Bunnie," explained Sally. "But we keep getting interrupted!"

"The princess is right," said Antoine. "Enough of this foolishness and small talk!" Antoine was a palace guard when Sally's father was the good king of Mobius. When Robotnik captured the king and took over the planet, Antoine remained by Sally's side. He was her most loyal servant, protector, and admirer.

"It seems to me," continued Antoine, "that planning our scouting mission is far more important than all this chatter. I think—"

"Move aside, Antoine," said Sonic, brushing past the stuffy guard. "All this talking is getting us nowhere. Let's start jamming on our planning!"

Antoine clenched his teeth and grumbled. Sally just rolled her eyes and sighed. "All right," said the princess. "Let's get down to business."

Chapter

3

The next morning, Bunnie, Sally, Antoine, and Rotor left Knothole Village and went on a scouting mission. The Freedom Fighters always took turns going on scouting missions. Since Sonic had gone out the day before, he stayed behind in Knothole Village as the others went on their way.

"This will be a good chance for me to test my new swatbot detector," said Rotor.

"Let's hope we don't need it," said Sally.

"Have no fear, your highness," said Antoine. "I am here to protect you."

"Enough talking, y'all," said Bunnie. "The wicked wastelands of Mobius await us!"

"Thanks, Bunnie," replied Sally, with a shiver. "You make me feel so much better!"

The small band of Freedom Fighters soon reached the edge of the Great Forest. Before them stretched the empty plains of Mobius.

"Let's go, Freedom Fighters," said Sally. "Quickly and quietly."

Sally and Antoine took the lead, with Bunnie and Rotor guarding the rear. The small group moved swiftly, covering the plains that bordered the Great Forest.

"How's your detector working, Rotor?" asked Bunnie.

Rotor looked at the gadget. Its antennae twirled and a green light blinked slowly.

"So far so good, Bunnie," replied Rotor. "If this green light turns red, that means there are swatbots in the area. I hope it stays green all day."

"Me too, Rotor," said Bunnie grimly. "Me too."

Up ahead, Sally and Antoine paused and looked around.

"Mobius has certainly become a depressing place since Robotnik took over, your highness," said Antoine.

"We're going to change all that one day, Antoine," said Sally. "I give you my word."

Suddenly from behind them came a cry for help.

"Help! Princess! Antoine! Help!"

"It's Bunnie!" shouted Sally. "Come on!"

Sally and Antoine raced toward the cries. When they reached Bunnie and Rotor, they were horrified to see a squadron of Robotnik's buzzbombers—giant flying robotic bees—attacking from the sky.

The buzzbombers were firing energy blasts at Bunnie and Rotor, who had run for cover behind a boulder.

When Sally and Antoine arrived, several of the buzzbombers turned their attention to the newcomers. Sally and Antoine dove behind the giant rock that protected Bunnie and Rotor.

"Didn't your detector warn you about this, Rotor?" Sally asked when she and Antoine had joined the others.

"I'm sorry, your highness," moaned Rotor. "It was set for swatbots, not buzzbombers."

Suddenly the light on Rotor's detector turned from green to red. "Uh-oh, princess," stammered Rotor. "Now I think we've got swatbots too!"

Sally peeked over the top of the boulder. A team of ten swatbots stared at her.

"You-will-come-with-us," said the lead swatbot in a cold mechanical voice.

"In your dreams, pal," shouted Bunnie as she scampered over the boulder.

"Bunnie, no!" shouted Sally, but it was too late. Bunnie leaped from the boulder right onto a swatbot's head.

"You leave us alone!" screamed Bunnie as she pounded on the swatbot.

"Release-me-traitor!" said the swatbot, who reached up and grabbed Bunnie.

"Let go of my friend!" yelled Sally. She dashed toward the swatbots.

"Come back, princess," called Antoine. "It's not safe."

When Sally reached the swatbot, it bent down and smacked her aside. She landed ten feet away.

"Princess!" shouted Antoine, dashing to Sally's side.

Meanwhile, Rotor had his tools out and was frantically working on his swatbot detector. "If I can reverse the electrical current that detects incoming swatbots, maybe I can send an outgoing signal *to* the swatbots and overload their circuits!"

Rotor finished his tinkering and powered up his device. A high, shrill whine filled the air. Then a swatbot exploded.

"It's working!" shouted Rotor with glee.

"Evacuate!" cried the lead swatbot. "New-weapon! Dangerous-to-our-existence! Evacuate!"

Within seconds the swatbots were gone. Rotor ran over to where Antoine was helping Sally to her feet.

"Are you all right, Sally?" asked Rotor.

"Yes, I'm fine," she replied. "But where's Bunnie?"

Rotor and Antoine looked around. There was no sign of Bunnie.

"The swatbots must have taken her!" cried Sally. "Let's get back to Knothole. We've got to tell Sonic!"

A short while later Sally, Antoine, and Rotor glided down the entrance slide to Knothole Village.

"Hey, Sal!" said Sonic when the three Freedom Fighters hit the hay pile at the bottom of the slide. "How was the scouting mission?"

"The swatbots have taken Bunnie," cried Sally. "I'm afraid Robotnik will put her into his Ro-Bo-Machine. Then she'll be just another one of his mindless robots!"

Sonic grew serious. "This calls for a Super Sonic rescue mission," he said, ready to zoom right off. "I'm juicing!"

"No. Wait, Sonic," ordered Sally, grabbing his arm. "You can't just rush right off to Robotropolis. We've got to come up with a plan. We've got to rescue Bunnie!"

Chapter
4

Deep in Robotropolis two swatbots carried Bunnie Rabbit, each holding one of her arms.

"Let me go!" shouted Bunnie, kicking at the large metal soldiers. Her cries echoed down the damp, dark hallway.

The swatbots soon came to a row of jail cells. Bunnie looked in horror at the prisoners who were locked in the cells. They looked tired and hungry. They had lost all hope of ever being freed.

Robotnik stood in front of an open cell. Cluck perched on his shoulder. The swatbots threw Bunnie into the empty cell, then locked the heavy iron door.

"I hope you like our pleasant accommodations, traitor," snarled Robotnik. "You're going to be here for a very long time."

Bunnie grabbed the bars on the cell door. "You'll never get away with this, Robotnik!" she shouted. "My friends will come to rescue me."

"Yes," snickered Robotnik, his evil laugh filling the dungeon. "That's exactly what I'm counting on. And when they do, I'll be ready for them!"

•••••

Back in Knothole Village, the Freedom Fighters were working on a rescue plan.

"We have to get inside Robotropolis," said Sonic. "Then we have to find Bunnie, rescue her, and destroy Robotnik's Ro-Bo-Machine."

"But Robotropolis is like a fortress," said Antoine. "Robotnik has swatbots patrolling everywhere. How do we even get inside that terrible place?"

"I've got an idea," said Sally. "Uncle Chuck, do you think you could design a giant motorized robot that looks like Robotnik?"

Uncle Chuck looked at Sally in horror. "Why would I want to do that? One Robotnik, even normal size, is more than enough!"

"Here's my idea," replied Sally. "Robotnik is in love with himself, right? So if a giant robot that looked like him showed up, he'd just accept it without question. He'd think it was a tribute to his 'greatness.'"

Uncle Chuck nodded. "I see," he said. "Well, I suppose I could design something like that. But what good is it going to do?"

"Because when Robotnik takes the giant robot into Robotropolis, we'll be hiding inside!" explained Sally.

"Way past cool idea, Sally," cried Sonic.

"I'll start designing it right away," said Uncle Chuck.

"And I'll help you build it," added Rotor, pulling out his huge box of tools. Uncle Chuck and Rotor began building the giant robot.

"Your highness, I see a problem with this plan," said Antoine.

"You always see a problem, Antoine," said Sonic. "You worry too much about everything."

"And you just rush into things without thinking. You're always putting the princess in danger!" Antoine snapped back.

"Boys! Boys!" yelled Sally. "This isn't going to help. Antoine, what do you think is the problem with our plan?"

"Thank you, your highness," he replied, giving Sonic a dirty look. "Once we are inside Robotropolis, how will we find Bunnie and the Ro-Bo-Machine? The city is huge. It could take days to track them down. And the longer we take to find Bunnie and the Ro-Bo-Machine, the greater the chances of Robotnik's swatbots finding us!"

"Wait a minute!" said Sally. "Uncle Chuck has been inside Robotropolis. He's seen the jail cells *and* the Ro-Bo-Machine. Maybe he remembers where they are. That could save us a lot of time and trouble!"

Sally, Sonic, and Antoine found Uncle Chuck hard at work with Rotor.

"Uncle Chuck," began Sonic. "I hate to make you think about this again, but it's important for our mission. Do you remember where the Ro-Bo-Machine is located?"

Uncle Chuck's face turned pale. "Thinking about that place gives me a bad feeling in my stomach," he explained. "When you changed me back from my robot form with the magic power ring, all thoughts of that terrible experience disappeared. It's possible the information is buried deep in my memory, but I don't know how we could get at it."

"What if we used a power ring again?" asked Sally.

"It's worth a try," said Uncle Chuck, "if it can help save Bunnie from a robotic fate!"

"There's no time to lose," said Sonic. "I'm juicing!"

Sonic took off in a blur, racing to the power-ring pond. Tails was sitting at the edge of the pond. He liked to play there, waiting for the rings to come up to the surface.

"Hi, Sonic," said Tails when he saw his hero. "What's going on?"

"A very important mission, Tails," said Sonic. "And you can help."

"I can?" asked Tails. "Wow! What do I have to do?"

"We need a power ring," explained Sonic. "You can help me by grabbing it when it comes up to the surface."

"Okay, Sonic," replied Tails. "You've got it!"

Tails stared at the power-ring pond. Its smooth surface reflected his face like a mirror.

Suddenly a bubbling began on the surface, right in the middle of the pond. Tails's two tails began to spin. He lifted off the ground, and zoomed to the middle of the pond. He hovered just above the surface.

Within seconds, a power ring rose up to the surface. Tails reached down and snatched the ring from the pond.

"Got it, Sonic!" said Tails, beaming with pride.

He zipped back to shore and handed the ring to Sonic.

"Good work, Tails," said Sonic. "You're a real Freedom Fighter. Now I've got to juice. See you later!"

Sonic zoomed back to where Uncle Chuck was waiting with Sally.

"Here goes nothing," said Sonic as he held the ring over Uncle Chuck's head.

Uncle Chuck soon fell into a deep sleep. A bright glow shined from the ring, surrounding him. A few seconds later, images from his memory were projected onto a nearby wall.

Sally flipped on her portable computer, Nicole. "I'm saving all these images in Nicole's memory banks," said Sally.

An image of the inside of Robotropolis flashed on the wall.

"That's it," cried Sally. "That's exactly what we need!"

Sonic removed the power ring, and the glow stopped. Uncle Chuck woke up.

"Have you started yet, Sonic?" he asked.

"All done, Uncle Chuck!" said Sonic. "And we got the information we needed."

"Great," said Uncle Chuck. "I didn't feel a thing. Now I can get back to work on this giant robot."

"We've got what we need in Nicole's memory banks, Sonic," said Sally. "I think this plan is going to work."

Sonic slipped the power ring into his backpack. "This might come in handy later," he said.

"This mission still isn't going to be easy, princess," said Antoine.

Sally sighed. She knew Antoine was right.

Chapter
5

Uncle Chuck and Rotor worked nonstop for the next few days. Finally the giant Robotnik robot was completed. The Freedom Fighters all gathered to look at their secret weapon.

"Wow!" said Sonic. "That's one big ugly Robotnik!"

"Excellent job," praised Antoine. "It certainly looks like Robotnik."

"Even though I made it, just looking at it gives me the creeps," said Uncle Chuck.

"Let's hope Robotnik likes it enough to bring it into Robotropolis," said Sally.

"Can I go along on this mission, Sonic?" asked Tails.

"Not just yet, little guy," replied Sonic. "Besides, I need you here to look after Uncle Chuck and protect Knothole Village while we're gone."

"Okay, Sonic, whatever you say," said Tails.

"Let's get this ugly thing on the move!" said Sonic.

Sonic, Sally, Antoine, Rotor, and Muttski climbed inside the giant robot. Once inside, they all took seats. Rotor sat at the controls.

"Here goes," said Rotor starting the robot's engine. The huge creation began to walk forward. Rotor used a monitor on his control panel to see where he was going.

The giant robot picked up speed as the Freedom Fighters crossed the plains of Mobius. The huge steel gates of Robotropolis were soon in sight.

"Robotropolis straight ahead," called out Rotor when the frightful city appeared on his monitor.

"Slow it down, Rotor," ordered Sally. "Let's

approach the gate slowly and stop just in front of it."

Sitting at a security monitor deep within Robotropolis, Robotnik watched the arrival of the giant robot. Cluck and Snively looked on.

"Ah, Cluck, that would be Sonic and his friends hiding in that sorry likeness of me," said Robotnik. "Naturally I was *expecting* Sonic to come on a rescue mission. I suppose this robot statue of me is some sort of trick. I'll just let Sonic think his little plan has succeeded. Snively!"

"Yes, sir, Dr. Robotnik?" whimpered Snively.

"Have a team of swatbots bring that giant robot to the large cargo storage room," ordered Robotnik.

"Yes, your greatness," said Snively.

"This will be all too easy," snickered Robotnik.

Cluck squawked gleefully.

Outside the front gate of Robotropolis, the Freedom Fighters waited within the giant robot.

"What do we do now, Sal?" asked Sonic. "All this waiting around is driving me nuts!"

"Relax, Sonic," said Sally. "Not everything can be solved by using your Super Sonic Speed. Sometimes you just have to be patient."

Sonic shook his head and paced nervously inside the robot's cockpit.

Suddenly, a team of swatbots marched out of the main entrance to Robotropolis.

"We've got company, gang," announced Rotor.

"Everybody sit still," ordered Sally. "If this goes right, we should be escorted right into Robotropolis."

Following Robotnik's orders, the swatbots swung open the heavy gate and pushed the giant robot into the fortress city. Once inside, the Freedom Fighters watched their monitor closely. They were led down a narrow hallway until they came to the cargo storage room. The door slid open, and the robot was shoved inside. The swatbots then filed out, slamming the door behind them.

The Freedom Fighters were alone inside Robotropolis.

"It worked!" said Sally, as Rotor pushed open the door leading out of the robot.

"Way to go, Sal," said Sonic, as the Freedom Fighters climbed down to the cargo room's floor.

"What now, your highness?" asked Antoine.

Sally pulled her computer, Nicole, from her backpack. "Okay, Nicole," Sally began. "Let's project file 'Chuck.map' on that wall."

"Certainly, Sally," responded Nicole.

A light beamed from Nicole, projecting a map of Robotropolis on the wall. Antoine stood near the map, tracing the route to the jail cells.

"That's it," said Sonic. "We're ready to juice! It's time to rescue Bunnie!"

Sonic, Sally, Antoine, and Rotor banged their fists together and gave the thumbs up. This was the Freedom Fighter handshake. Muttski barked, showing that he was ready too.

"Let's do it to it!" shouted Sonic.

What the Freedom Fighters didn't know was that Robotnik was watching them on his monitor.

"I was right," said Robotnik. "My guests have arrived. Snively! The cage."

"Yes, sir," whined Snively. He pressed a button on the control panel.

In the cargo room, a huge steel cage fell from the ceiling. It hit the floor with a loud clang, landing right over the Freedom Fighters. Sonic and his friends were trapped!

Robotnik's voice boomed over a loudspeaker in the cargo room. "I've got you now, hedgehog!"

Chapter

6

"My plan worked perfectly, Cluck," said Robotnik with a laugh. On the monitor he saw Sonic and the other Freedom Fighters trapped inside his steel cage.

"Very well done, sir," added Snively, not wanting to be left out.

"Of course it's very well done, Snively," snapped Robotnik. "*I* did it!"

"Yes, sir," moaned Snively. "You did it."

"Now, Snively," continued Robotnik. "Send all my swatbots to the large cargo room to bring Sonic The Hedgehog to me."

"Very good, sir," sighed Snively. He switched on a microphone that was connected to speakers all over the city. "Attention all swatbots. By command of our supreme ruler, Dr. Robotnik, you are hereby ordered to report to the large cargo room. Bring Sonic The Hedgehog and his fellow traitors to Dr. Robotnik at once." Snively switched off the microphone.

"Nice touch, Snively," said Robotnik. "The 'fellow traitors' part."

"Thank you, sir," said Snively, delighted to receive any praise.

"Aark!" squawked Cluck jealously from Robotnik's shoulder.

Back in the cargo bay the Freedom Fighters paced within their steel trap.

"This was a setup," said Sally. "I'll bet Robotnik took Bunnie only to lure the rest of us here. He knew we'd come after her, and boy was he ready for us."

The door to the cargo room slid open and a team of swatbots stormed in.

"Oh, dear," cried Antoine. "We're finished!"

"Secure-hedgehog. Take-to-Dr.-Robotnik," said a swatbot.

"Enough talk," said Sonic. "It's time for a Super Sonic Spin to get us out of here!"

Sonic whirled into a Super Sonic Spin. He looked like a swirling blue buzz saw as he cut through the cage's bars. Within seconds, the Freedom Fighters were out of the cage.

Sonic and Rotor picked up the top of the cage and hurled it at the swatbots. The flying metal bars knocked the swatbots over like bowling pins.

"Come on, guys," said Sonic. "We are out of here!"

Led by Sonic, the Freedom Fighters dashed from the cargo room. Rotor switched on his swatbot detector. It immediately started blinking red, indicating swatbots in the area. "More swatbots are nearby," announced Rotor.

"Quickly," ordered Sally. "Let's hide until they pass."

The Freedom Fighters ducked behind a huge piece of machinery. A team of swatbots raced around a bend not far from where the Freedom Fighters were hiding.

"Oh, we're doomed for certain," moaned Antoine. Unfortunately he moaned a bit too loudly. The swatbots heard him.

"Traitors-located," said a swatbot. "Open-fire."

The swatbots began shooting energy blasts that narrowly missed the Freedom Fighters.

"Sit tight, guys," said Sonic. "It's juicing time for me!"

Sonic dashed from his hiding place and sped toward the swatbots.

"Bet you can't hit me, robot dudes," taunted Sonic. The swatbots fired, but Sonic outran each of their blasts.

"Now let's turn the tables on these metal morons," said Sonic. He continued speeding along, but this time Sonic weaved all around and in between the swatbots. "You guys need to take some extra target practice," said Sonic. "At each other!"

The swatbots fired at Sonic, but blew up each other instead. Sonic continuing racing from swatbot to swatbot until the shooting stopped.

"That takes care of them," said Sonic, dusting himself off.

"Help, Sonic, over here!" called Sally.

There was still one swatbot remaining. It had the Freedom Fighters cornered, its energy weapon aimed right at them.

"This calls for some Warp Sonic Speed," said Sonic, pulling the power ring from his backpack. He held the power ring over his head. It began to glow with golden energy.

Sonic zoomed over to the swatbot, then ran around and around it in a blinding blue circle.

The swatbot's head began to spin, trying to follow Sonic. Its head spun so fast that it began to short circuit. Sparks and flames flew from its head.

Sonic rounded up his friends. "Hang on to me," he said, as they formed a chain, with Sonic at the lead. Still glowing with Warp Sonic Power from the power ring, Sonic and the others raced off, just as the last swatbot exploded into a million pieces.

The Freedom Fighters raced through Robotropolis.

"Nice work, Sonic," said Rotor when they came to a stop.

Sally projected the Robotropolis map from Nicole onto a wall. "According to the map, Bunnie's cell should be right around the next corridor."

"Let's hurry," said Antoine, looking over his shoulder for any more swatbots.

Seconds later they arrived at the jail cells. All the cells they passed were empty.

"Bunnie should be right in there," said Sally, pointing ahead.

But when the Freedom Fighters looked in Bunnie's cell, it was empty too.

"She's gone!" shouted Antoine in a panic.

"We're too late!" said Sally. "Robotnik's already taken her to his Ro-Bo-Machine!"

Chapter
7

"Quick, Nicole," shouted Sally, pulling out her computer. "Project the Robotropolis map onto the wall. We've got to find our way to the Ro-Bo-Machine."

Nicole projected a light beam onto the wall, but something was wrong. The image was all fuzzy. *"I'm sorry, Sally,"* said Nicole. *"The image of the Ro-Bo-Machine I got from Uncle Chuck's mind is unclear. I can't project the exact route for you."*

"Now what do we do?" moaned Antoine.

Muttski began barking.

"What is it, boy?" asked Sonic.

Muttski dashed off down the hall, barking as he ran.

"I'll bet he's picked up Bunnie's scent," cried Sally. "Come on. Let's follow him!"

From his control room, Robotnik watched on his monitor as the Freedom Fighters made their way toward the Ro-Bo-Machine.

"My cage couldn't hold you," he cackled. "But that's all right. Come to my machine, hedgehog. Then I'll turn you and your friends into my robot servants."

Sonic and the others followed Muttski, making their way through the twisting passageways of Robotropolis. Muttski was hot on Bunnie's trail. They soon came to a steel door at the end of a hallway. Muttski jumped up and down and barked loudly.

"That must be the entrance to the machine room," said Sally. "Good work, Muttski!"

"Ready for some first-class rescuing?" asked Sonic. "Then here we go!"

Suddenly the ceiling slid open, and a team of swatbots dropped down from above. "Freeze-traitors," shouted the lead swatbot.

"Oh, no," cried Antoine. "Another trap!"

Rotor pulled out his swatbot detector. He set it to the signal that would destroy the swatbots.

"This will slow them down," said Rotor. But before he could activate the device, a swatbot fired his energy blaster and knocked the device from Rotor's hand. The detector hit the floor and burst into flames, then exploded.

A second team of swatbots arrived. The Freedom Fighters were completely surrounded.

Sonic and his friends were led into a large room. In the center of the room sat Robotnik's Ro-Bo-Machine.

"Welcome!" boomed Robotnik's voice over a loudspeaker. The Freedom Fighters spotted Robotnik through a thick glass window. He sat in his control room with Cluck perched on his shoulder and Snively standing ready by his side.

"You can all be my guests as we watch your friend change into a robot. But don't be jealous. You'll each have your own turn to be roboticized!

Ha, ha, ha!" Robotnik laughed wickedly. "Snively! Bring in the prisoner."

"Yes, Dr. Robotnik," whimpered Snively. Snively switched on his microphone. "Attention swatbot unit 11. Bring in the prisoner."

Cluck squawked loudly.

"Faster, Snively," shouted Robotnik. "Cluck grows impatient!"

Snively shot a nasty glance at Cluck. "As you wish, sir," he mumbled.

The door to the large room slid open. In came Bunnie Rabbit carried by two swatbot guards.

"Look!" cried Sally. "It's Bunnie!"

"Let me go!" shouted Bunnie, kicking at the swatbots that held her.

The Freedom Fighters looked on in horror as Bunnie was put into the Ro-Bo-Machine. The glass dome dropped from the ceiling. Blue rings of light flashed and a droning hum filled the room. The process of turning Bunnie into a robot had begun.

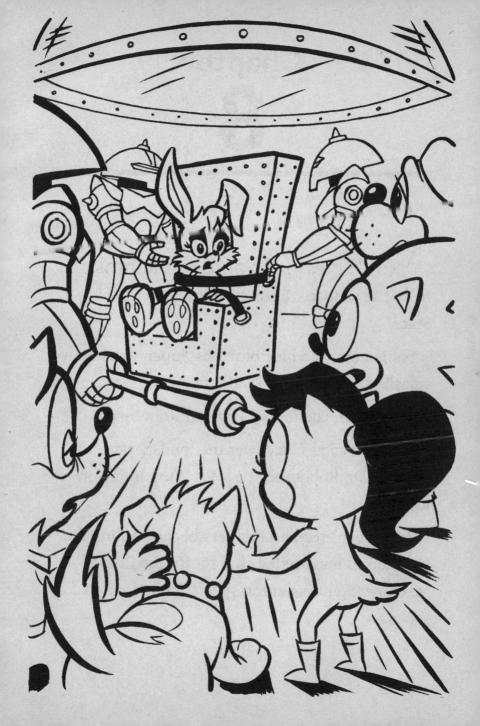

Chapter
8

"No!" screamed Sonic, as he broke free of a swatbot. "This calls for a Super Sonic Spin!"

Sonic became a blue blur. His Super Sonic Spin smashed swatbot after swatbot.

"Stop him, you fools!" ordered Robotnik.

Snively's voice came over the loudspeaker. "By order of Dr. Robotnik," he said. "Stop him, you fools!"

The other Freedom Fighters began battling the swatbots. Sonic headed straight for the Ro-Bo-Machine. Spinning at top speed, Sonic shattered the glass.

Sonic pulled Bunnie from the machine's seat. She was unconscious. She was also half changed. Her body, legs, and left arm had already become mechanical. Her head and right arm were still those of a living rabbit.

"At least they didn't change her head," said Sally, gratefully. "I only hope her mind is still working."

In the control room Robotnik was furious. "Do something, Snively!" he shouted.

"I'm trying, sir," said Snively, frantically pushing buttons. "But it seems that when Sonic smashed the glass, the entire power circuit fused. The doors won't open. We can't get out of this control room!"

Rotor set to work crossing the circuits in the Ro-Bo-Machine. He attached a portable generator he had brought along just for this purpose. "All set," said Rotor.

"Then let 'er rip, Rotor," said Sonic.

Rotor switched on the generator. Energy began to build up at an incredible rate. "The Ro-Bo-Machine is going to blow sky-high any second," said Rotor.

"I don't plan on sticking around to see it, Rotor," replied Sonic. He picked up the still-unconscious Bunnie in his arms. "Okay, Freedom Fighters, time to juice!"

Carrying Bunnie, Sonic led the Freedom Fighters out of the Ro-Bo-Machine room and down a hallway.

The generator sent a tremendous boost of power into the machine, and the whole thing exploded with a thunderous roar. Robotnik's Ro-Bo-Machine was destroyed!

The glass between the machine room and Robotnik's control room shattered. The force of the explosion sent Robotnik, Snively, and Cluck flying backwards. They landed in a pile, one on top of another.

"Get off of me, you stupid chicken," shouted Snively.

Cluck squawked angrily.

"This is all your fault, Snively," yelled Robotnik.

"My fault, sir?" replied Snively. "I think your

swatbots failed you, Dr. Robotnik. Not to mention your machine and your idiotic chicken!"

"Oh, shut up, Snively," snapped Robotnik. "Get your foot off my face and help me up! We still have one final surprise for the intruders!"

"Yes, sir," sighed Snively, getting to his feet.

The Freedom Fighters sped down a narrow passageway. "Which way, Sal?" asked Sonic.

Sally pulled Nicole from her backpack. The computer projected a map onto the wall. "This way," said Sally, pointing. "We're almost out of here."

The Freedom Fighters reached the main gate to Robotropolis. "Freedom is in sight," shouted Sonic.

Suddenly a large steel wall dropped in front of them, blocking their path.

"What do we do now?" asked Antoine.

"Hey, y'all, what's going on?" It was Bunnie. She was awake!

"Bunnie!" cried Sally. "Are you all right?"

Bunnie looked down at her new robot body. "What have they done to me?" she cried. "I'm half-rabbit, half-robot!"

"I'm sorry, Bunnie," said Sally. "I wish we had gotten there sooner."

"We've still got to get out of Robotropolis," Sonic reminded the others.

"This just makes me so mad," screamed Bunnie. "I feel like kicking something."

Bunnie kicked the steel wall with her new robotic leg. *BAM!* The wall smashed open, leaving a big hole.

"Hmm," said Bunnie, feeling a little better. "Maybe there *is* something good about this robot thing!"

One by one the Freedom Fighters slipped through the opening in the wall. They were soon outside Robotropolis.

"Come on," said Sonic. "Let's juice back to the Great Forest."

Epilogue

The Freedom Fighters soon returned to Knothole Village. They were greeted by Uncle Chuck and Tails.

"Way to go, Sonic," said Tails. "You're the best!"

"Nice bit of rescuing, my boy," added Uncle Chuck.

"Thanks, guys," said Sonic. "But we've still got work to do. I've got to try to restore Bunnie to normal with a power ring."

"It worked for Muttski and me," said Uncle Chuck.

"I just hope it works for Bunnie," said Sally.

Sonic pulled the power ring from his backpack.

"Let 'er rip, sugar," said Bunnie closing her eyes tightly.

Golden light beamed from the ring and surrounded Bunnie. When the light stopped, Bunnie looked the same.

"What happened, Sonic?" asked Sally. "She's still half robot!"

"It didn't work," said Sonic. "Robotnik must have changed his Ro-Bo-Machine so that the power rings have no effect on people once he's roboticized them!"

"That's, okay, Sonic," said Bunnie. "You still got me out of that terrible place. And Robotnik may have made me half robot, but there's one thing he could never change, and that's my heart. I'm just thankful I have such good friends. I love everyone in my Freedom Fighter family."

Bunnie hugged each of her friends. "Besides," she said, "with my robot arm and legs, I'm ready to go back there and kick some Robotnik butt!"

"You know, Bunnie," said Sonic. "I think from now on we should call you Bunnie Rabbot. After all, you're half-rabbit, half-robot!"

Everyone laughed as they headed off to celebrate Bunnie's rescue.

Now that Bunnie was safe, the Freedom Fighters could once again work together to help free their planet!

• •